THE Hogan that Great-Grandfather Built

Written by
Nancy Bo Flood

Illustrated by
Peterson Yazzie

Library of Congress Cataloging-in-Publication Data

Flood, Nancy Bo.
 The Hogan that Great-Grandfather Built / written by Nancy Bo Flood ; illustrated by Peterson Yazzie ; edited by Jessie Ruffenach.--
1st ed.

 ISBN 13: 978-1-893354-97-5
(hardcover : alk. paper)

Edited by Jessie Ruffenach
Designed by Corey Begay

Printed in the United States of America

Third Printing, First Edition
20 19 18 17 16 15 14 10 9 8 7 6 5 4 3

The paper used in this publication meets the minimum requirements of the American National Standard for Information Sciences
— Permanence of Paper for Printed Library Materials, ANSI Z39.48-1984.

Salina Bookshelf, Inc.
Flagstaff, Arizona 86001
www.salinabookshelf.com

Dedication

To our grandchildren, our new generation of "home".

Archer Tennyson Henry, Morris Antonio Storm, Culley Dean Gilbert, Rowan Edward Herb, and Eva Kay Berniar

This is our home, our Navajo hogan,
that long, long ago, Great-Grandfather Jack
built with his hands out of earth, water, and trees.

This is my grandmother
who lives in our hogan.

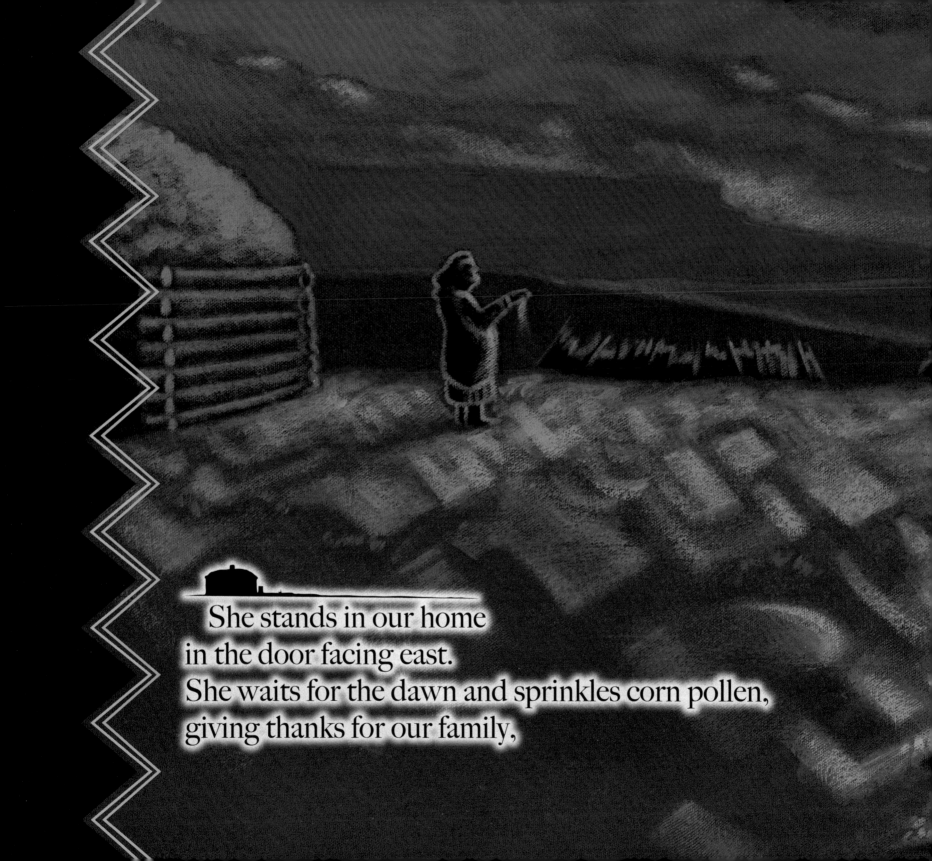

She stands in our home
in the door facing east.
She waits for the dawn and sprinkles corn pollen,
giving thanks for our family,

the canyons, the mesas,
and for this home,
our Navajo hogan,
that long, long ago,
Great-Grandfather Jack
built with his hands
out of earth, water, and trees.

This is my sister
who runs toward the sun
as it rises each morning.

She welcomes the Holy Ones
blessing the sunrise,
while Grandmother waits at the door
facing east of our home,

our Navajo hogan, that long, long ago,
Great-Grandfather Jack built
with his hands out of
earth, water, and trees.

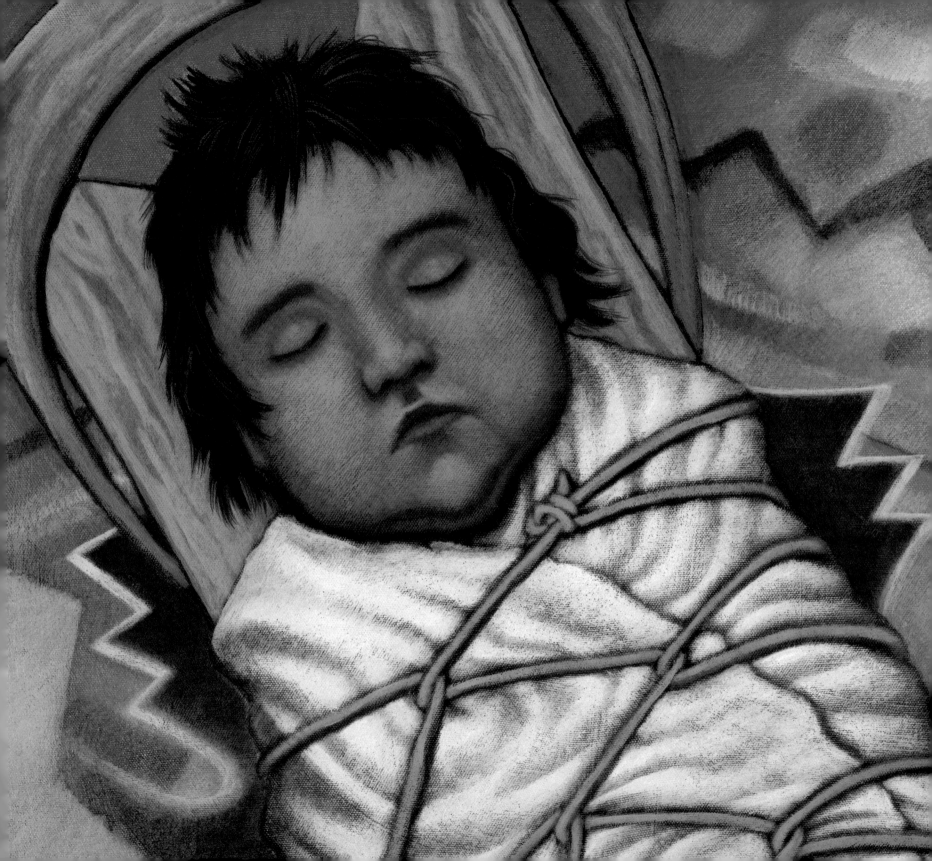

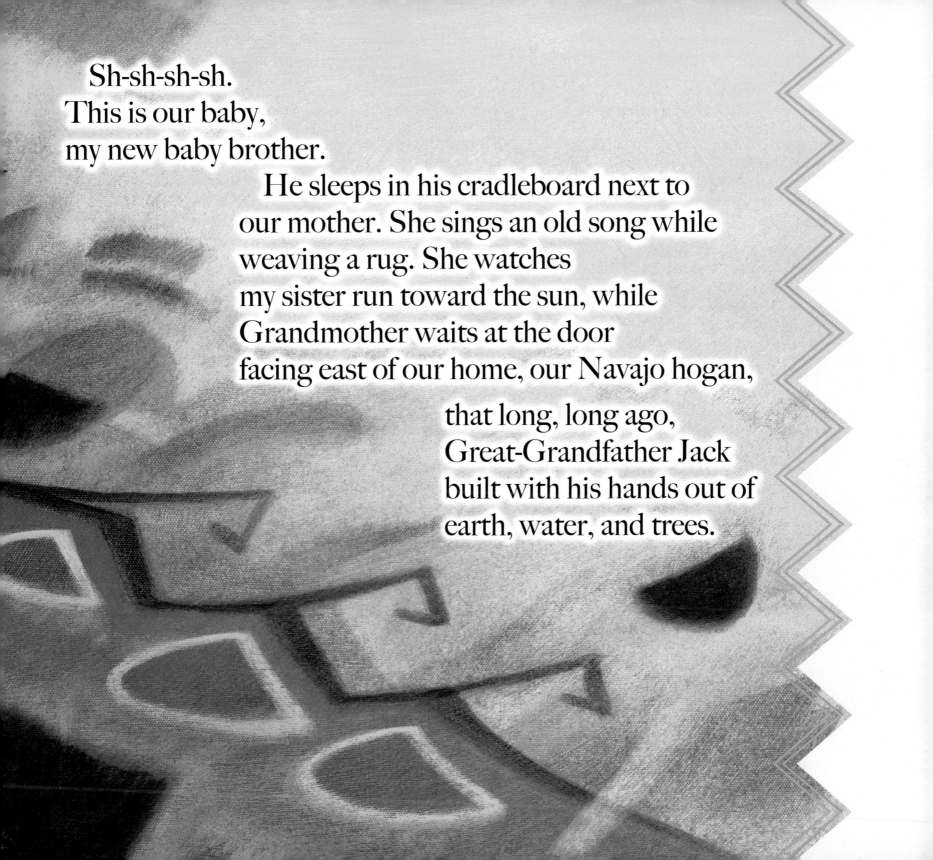

Sh-sh-sh-sh.
This is our baby,
my new baby brother.
He sleeps in his cradleboard next to
our mother. She sings an old song while
weaving a rug. She watches
my sister run toward the sun, while
Grandmother waits at the door
facing east of our home, our Navajo hogan,

that long, long ago,
Great-Grandfather Jack
built with his hands out of
earth, water, and trees.

This is my Grandfather.
He stacks wood for the winter
that will warm our hogan
when chilly winds blow.

Then Grandfather's voice will soften the darkness
As he teaches the star names and shows us
the string games,

telling us stories of how we began,
and of our home, our Navajo hogan,
that long, long ago, Great-Grandfather Jack
built with his hands
out of earth, water, and trees.

What do I hear that is
roaring and rumbling?

A pick-up truck rattles,
sending sand flying.

Father is home,
back from work
and from shopping!

He brings food and supplies,
and maybe...

surprises –
back to our home, our Navajo hogan,
Where mother weaves,
Baby sleeps,

Grandmother waits,
Grandfather works –
and sister and me?

We race
over to Father.

"I'm home!" He is laughing. Father is back, here in
our home, our Navajo hogan, that long, long ago,

Great-Grandfather Jack
built with his hands out of
earth, water, and trees.

Father smiles at my brother
and nods to my mother.
I climb in the back
of our blue pick-up truck.

Bags and more bags
I hand to my sister.
Grandmother calls,

"The fire is hot."
Fry bread is sizzling,
mutton stew bubbles.

This is my family
walking in beauty,
Here in our home,
our Navajo hogan,
that long, long ago,
Great-Grandfather Jack

built with his hands out of earth, water, and trees.

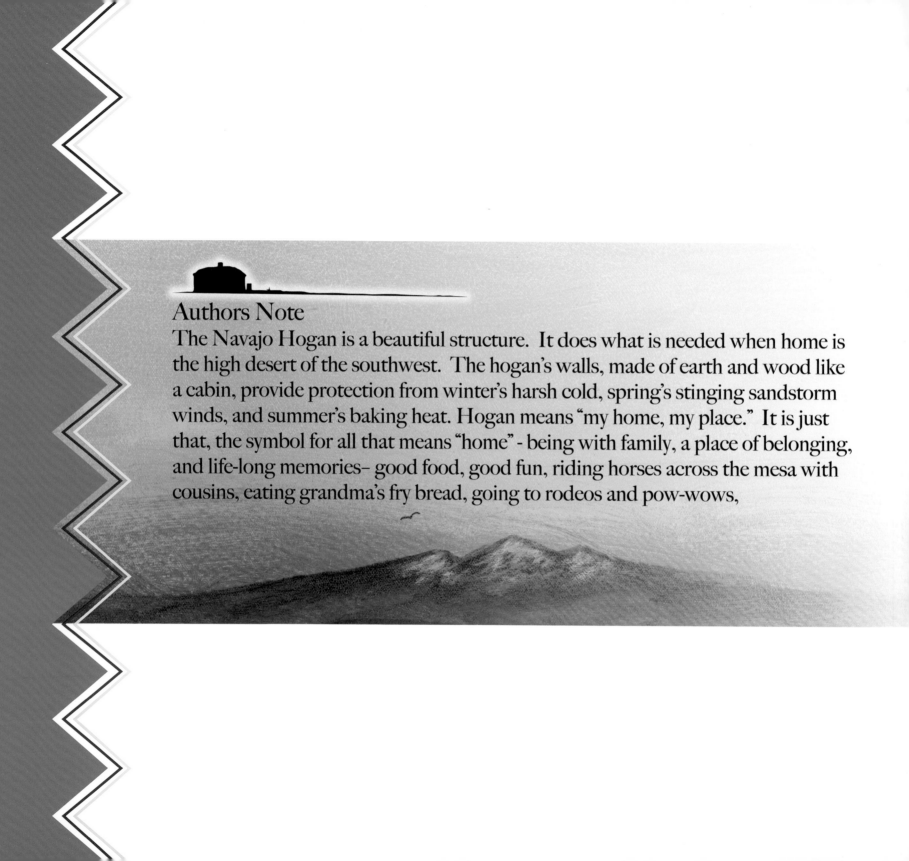

Authors Note

The Navajo Hogan is a beautiful structure. It does what is needed when home is the high desert of the southwest. The hogan's walls, made of earth and wood like a cabin, provide protection from winter's harsh cold, spring's stinging sandstorm winds, and summer's baking heat. Hogan means "my home, my place." It is just that, the symbol for all that means "home" - being with family, a place of belonging, and life-long memories– good food, good fun, riding horses across the mesa with cousins, eating grandma's fry bread, going to rodeos and pow-wows, spending dark, star-filled nights at sheep camp, and also a place of healing and celebrating coming-of-age or getting married. Even today, Navajo families who live off the Reservation in small towns or big cities, in western-style houses, condominiums, or high-rise apartments, return to their ancestral land on the Navajo Nation, to the family Hogan, for celebrations and for healing. The Hogan continues to mean home.